Our Emotions and Behaviour

I Hate Everything!

Written by Sue Graves

Illustrated by

Desideria Guicciardini

FRANKLIN WATTS

LONDON • SYDNEY

Last night, Sam couldn't sleep because Charlie was **crying**.

Sam got cross. He **hated** it when Charlie cried.

In the morning, Sam wanted to play football with Dad. But Dad was **busy**.

Dad said he would play later.
Sam wanted Dad to play **now**.
He got **cross**.

At lunchtime, Dad gave Sam some carrots. But Sam **hated** carrots. Dad said they would make him **big and strong**.

Sam said he didn't want
to be big and strong **ever!**
He got **very cross.**

Dad told Sam to go to his room and **calm down**.

But Sam didn't want to go to his room.
He didn't want **to calm down.**

In the afternoon, Sam went to Archie's **party.** He wanted the cake with the cherry on top, but Ellie took it.

Sam got **cross**. He **pushed** Ellie so hard she dropped the cake.

Then everyone played "Musical Chairs".
When the music stopped, Sam wasn't
fast enough. He didn't get a chair.
Archie said Sam was **out**.
Sam said he **wasn't out** at all.

"I hate everything!" Sam shouted.
He stamped his feet.
Everyone was **cross** with Sam for
spoiling the party.

Aunty Jen took Sam outside. She said when she felt cross she took a **deep breath** and counted slowly to ten.

Sam took a **deep breath.** He counted **slowly** to ten. Soon, he started to feel better. He didn't feel so cross any more.

Aunty Jen told Sam there were lots of other things he could do when he felt **cross**. Sam had a think about what he could do.

He said he could **read a book**... or **tell someone**... or **run** round the garden ... or **play** with his dog, Monty.
Aunty Jen said these were all good ideas.

Sam wished that he had not spoiled Archie's party.

He told everyone he was **sorry**.

Then everyone played "Hide and Seek". Everyone ran and hid. Archie counted to **ten**.

Then he looked...and looked... and the first person he found was Sam! And Sam...

didn't get **cross** at all!

Can you tell the story of what happens when George has to have his hair cut?

How do you think George felt before he had
his hair cut? How did he feel afterwards?

A note about sharing this book

The *Our Emotions and Behaviour* series has been developed to provide a starting point for further discussion on children's feelings and behaviour, both in relation to themselves and to other people.

I Hate Everything!
This story explores, in a reassuring way, some typical situations that people dislike. It demonstrates how to cope in such situations and how to interact successfully with others.

The book aims to encourage children to have a developing awareness of behavioural expectations in different settings. It also invites children to begin to consider the consequences of their words and actions for themselves and others.

Storyboard puzzle
The wordless storyboard on pages 26 and 27 provides an opportunity for speaking and listening. Children are encouraged to tell the story illustrated in the panels: George hates having his hair cut and makes an awful fuss. But when he arrives at the salon, he is diverted by the idea of driving the car. In the end, he is pleasantly surprised to find that having a haircut can, in fact, be a fun experience.

How to use the book
The book is designed for adults to share with either an individual child or a group of children, and as a starting point for discussion.

The book also provides visual support and repeated words and phrases to build confidence in children who are starting to read on their own.

Before reading the story
Choose a time to read when you and the children are relaxed and have time to share the story.

Spend time looking at the illustrations and talk about what the book may be about before reading it together.

After reading, talk about the book with the children:

- What was it about? What things do the children hate? Do they all hate similar things? How do they cope when they have to deal with something they don't enjoy? Encourage the children to talk about their experiences.

- Do the children have things in common that they hate? Examples might be having to go to bed on time or eating up all their food. Encourage the children to talk not only about why they hate doing these things, but also about why it is important that they do them.

- Extend this by talking about other things that children hate, such as trying new foods, or new experiences. Have the children found that once something has been tried they have in fact changed their opinion? Point out that it is a good idea always to try something rather than to decide that they hate it.

- Spend time talking to the children about other words they might use instead of "hate" when describing situations they dislike. Examples might be feeling annoyed at having to tidy their bedrooms or having to entertain a younger brother or sister. They may feel anxious about dark places or creepy crawlies. Encourage the children to use new words to describe their feelings.

- Look at the end of the story again. Sam felt much happier when he laughed about being found first in the Hide and Seek game instead of getting angry. Why do the children think he felt happier with this new attitude?

- Look at the storyboard puzzle. Ask the children to tell the story in their own words. Why do they think George didn't want to have his hair cut? Do the children think he enjoyed the experience after all? Do they think he felt more comfortable after his hair was cut than before? Why? Do the children like having their hair cut? Why or why not? Encourage the children to talk about their own experiences.

Ask the children to draw something they dislike and something they love.

Encourage them to talk about their drawings during group time. Encourage them also to tell the others the strategies they employ to help them when they feel cross about something.

This edition 2015

First published in 2013 by
Franklin Watts
338 Euston Road
London
NW1 3BH

Franklin Watts Australia
Level 17/207 Kent Street
Sydney
NSW 2000

A CIP catalogue record for this book is available
from the British Library.

ISBN 978 1 4451 3899 2

Editor: Jackie Hamley
Designer: Peter Scoulding

Printed in China

Franklin Watts is a division of
Hachette Children's Books,
an Hachette UK company.
www.hachette.co.uk